APR 0 3 2019

NO LONGER PROPERTY OF
SEATTLE PUBLIC LIBRARY

Text copyright © 2019 by Wendy Greenley Illustrations copyright © 2019 by Paolo Domeniconi Edited by Amy Novesky; designed by Rita Marshall
Published in 2019 by Creative Editions P.O. Box 227, Mankato, MN 56002 USA Creative Editions is an imprint of The Creative Company www.thecreativecompany.us
All rights reserved. No part of the contents of this book may be reproduced by any means without the written permission of the publisher.
Printed in China.
Library of Congress Cataloging-in-Publication Data Names: Greenley, Wendy, author. / Domeniconi, Paolo, illustrator. Title: Lola shapes the sky / by Wendy Greenley; illustrated by Paolo Domeniconi. Summary: A cloud with a mind of her own and a gift for making awe-inspiring shapes encourages her friends to go beyond their practical functions and expand their imaginative horizons. Identifiers: LCCN 2018019494 / ISBN 978-1-56846-319-3 Subjects: CYAC: Clouds—Fiction. / Self-acceptance—Fiction.
Classification: LCC PZ7.1.G7403 Lo 2019 / DDC [E]—dc23 First edition 9 8 7 6 5 4 3 2 1

Lola Shapes the Sky

Wendy Greenley illustrated by Paolo Domeniconi

Creative Editions

formed on a fresh, wild wind.
Her one-of-a-kind outline blew
the other clouds away.

"Who wants to make a shape with me?" Lola asked.

"Clouds make weather, not shapes," said Thor.

The other clouds bobbed in agreement. It had always been this way.

"Time for shade!" Cyrus called, zooming high across the sky.
As the other clouds quickened and thickened—
Lola lengthened and looped.
"Look! I'm a snake! Sssssss!" she hissed in jest.

"Shape up, Lola!" Thor rumbled. "Time for rain."

Lola darkened. She strained. Her edges curled and swirled.

As the other clouds splish-splooshed—

Lola leaped.

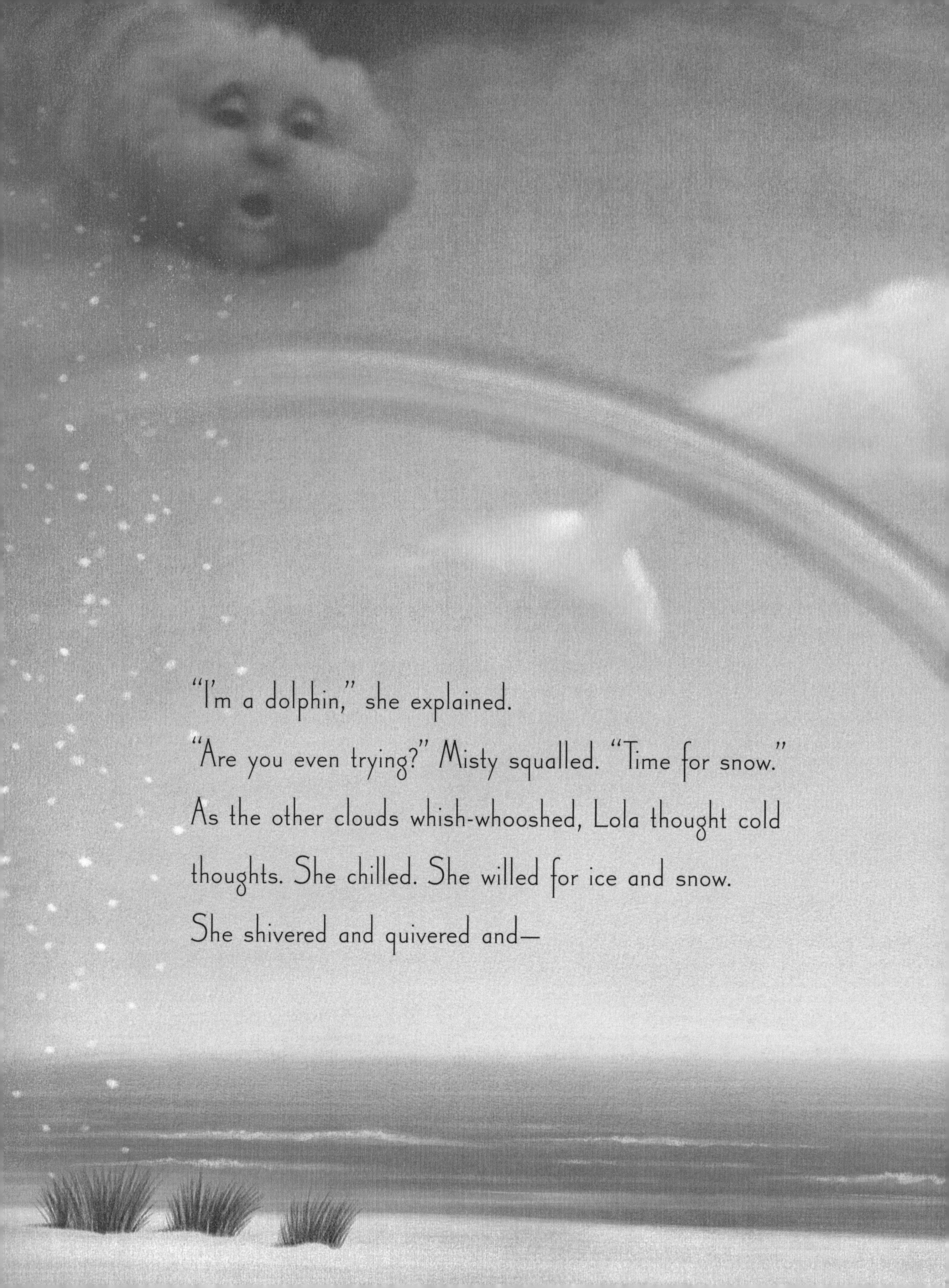

"I'm a dolphin," she explained.

"Are you even trying?" Misty squalled. "Time for snow."

As the other clouds whish-whooshed, Lola thought cold thoughts. She chilled. She willed for ice and snow. She shivered and quivered and—

"Look at ME!"

"You're the worst cloud ever!" howled Thor.

"You didn't make shade or rain OR snow.

Maybe you should just—evaporate."

Lola watched the other clouds sail away.
It was true. She hadn't made shade or
rain or snow.
Was she the worst cloud ever?

Feeling low, Lola drifted toward a
strange sound—
A *clap-a-clap!* Whoo-hoo! *Clap-a-clap!*
sound . . . and a shout.
"There! Look up!"

Lola twisted.

She twirled.

She mirrored the ground, and waited. . . .

Faces beamed skyward.

Lola steamed after the other clouds.

"I may not be a weather-maker!" she shouted,

"but I can be ferocious . . .

humorous . . .

gorgeous."

Thor ballooned twice in size.

"What good is THAT?" he bellowed.

"Look down," said Lola.

"They're waiting for weather." Thor stormed off.

"Are you sure?" Lola asked.

And that's when she shaped—

a pillowy, billowy masterpiece.

"Ooh!" The sound rose from the ground.

The other clouds gathered. "Make more shapes, Lola!"

"I'm a croco-plane!"

"I'm a tuba-playing ballerina."

"Make room for the two-headed
kangasaurus!"

"Show *us* how!" Misty begged.

Lola got to work.

The other clouds fluffed and puffed.

All but one.

Thor flashed wildly, and—*BOOM!*—
his thunderclaps shook the ground.

"Bravo, Lola!" Thor clapped.
"You *are* one of a kind."

From that day on, clouds made weather *and* shapes.

Sometimes at the same time!

"Anybody know tomorrow's forecast?" Thor asked.

"Clouds. Lots and lots of clouds," said Lola.

"The sky's the limit!"

All about Clouds

Clouds are vital to life on Earth. Without clouds, there would be no shade, no rain, no snow.

Clouds form when water vapor in the air condenses onto tiny specks of dust, like the water that appears on the bathroom mirror when you shower.

No two clouds are exactly the same.

Cirrus (*SEER-uss*) clouds are made of ice. Formed high in the sky, these thin, wispy clouds are usually the fastest clouds, powered by winds at 100 miles (161 km) per hour! They look like they're standing still because they're so far away. Cirrus clouds often mean good weather or that a change in the weather is coming.

Stratus (*STRAH-tuss*) clouds cover the sky like a gray blanket! Near the ground, stratus clouds are called fog. Stratus clouds bring drizzle or snow, or it may just be a dry, dull day.

Cumulus (*KYOO-myoo-luss*) clouds are clumpy clouds with sky visible around them. They look like the top of a head of cauliflower, or cotton balls or popcorn floating in air. Thunderstorms develop from cumulus clouds with a flat base that reach high into the sky (called cumulonimbus).